THE SKYWRITER

DENNIS HASELEY

Illustrated by **DENNIS NOLAN**

A NEAL PORTER BOOK · ROARING BROOK PRESS · NEW YORK

Text copyright © 2008 by Dennis Haseley
Artwork copyright © 2008 by Dennis Nolan
Published by Roaring Brook Press
Roaring Brook Press is a division of Holtzbrinck Publishing Holdings Limited Partnership
175 Fifth Avenue, New York, New York 10010
www.roaringbrookpress.com

Library of Congress Cataloging-in-Publication Data
Haseley, Dennis, 1950-
The skywriter / Dennis Haseley ; illustrated by Dennis Nolan.—1st ed.
p. cm.
"A Neal Porter Book"
Summary: Although Charles grows too old for conversations and adventures with a toy soldier, baker, and airplane man,
he hopes that his old friends might take his new baby brother to a far-off land one day.
ISBN-13: 978-1-59643-252-9   ISBN-10: 1-59643-252-7
[1. Toys—Fiction. 2. Growth—Fiction. 3. Brothers and sisters—Fiction.]
I. Nolan, Dennis, ill. II. Title.
PZ7.N678Sky 2008   [E]—dc22   2007044053

Roaring Brook Press books are available for special promotions and premiums.
For details contact: Director of Special Markets, Holtzbrinck Publishers.

First Edition September 2008
Book design by Barbara Grzeslo
Printed in China

1 3 5 7 9 10 8 6 4 2

For Connor
—D. H.

For Jamie and Holly
—D. N.

Charles was kneeling by the dollhouse. He was talking to the figures, and they were talking back. He was just a little boy then.

"Come on," he said to the soldier. "Let's go over there!"

"I'll come, too," said the baker.

"We'll all fly over," said the airplane man. "And I'll do the loop the loop. I'll write letters in the sky."

"And will we go on adventures?" asked Charles.

"We will," said the airplane man. "I'll take you to a far-off land. Where everything's warm and everything shines. Where little people are as tall as trees."

"And what will you write in the sky?" Charles asked.

"HERE WE GO," said the airplane man.

"Let's go now," said Charles.

But they didn't answer him. He turned and saw his sister had come into the room. She was five years older.

"What are you doing?" she asked.

"Playing with them," he said. When he turned back to look, it seemed the soldier had moved inches forward.

She came up next to him. "And what were they talking about?"

"About an adventure," he said. "Didn't you hear?"

She shook her head.

"They told me about it," he said, looking back to them.

"Of course they did," she said. And before she left, she held each one in her hand for a moment.

When she was gone, the soldier boy said, "Yes, let's all fly."
"Flyyyy," said the airplane man.
"Make us flyyyy," said the baker.
And they all flew toward the far-off land.

A year passed, and then another. Sometimes Charles played with the little figures, but more often now he didn't. He couldn't remember when it was that he had stopped speaking to them, and when they had grown silent in turn. But it didn't matter so much now, because there was baseball, and friends on the block.

But once, when he was playing ball, the pitcher was standing still on the mound. And when Charles looked again, he was several steps forward. And another time, when he was alone in a field, he heard the buzz of an engine above him in the sky. When he stopped and looked up, he saw a tiny plane that looked just like the airplane man's. Doing the loop the loop. And writing letters in smoke that drifted and blurred. Did they say,

HERE WE GO . . .?

Then he thought of the land where everything shone, and little people grew as tall as trees.

A baby brother was coming to their family, and he would need the room they used to play in.

"You don't mind?" asked his mother.

Charles shook his head. "I don't mind," he said.

But that night he had a dream of an airplane that tipped its wings; and when he asked his mother in the morning why airplanes did such a thing, she smiled and said, "It's the way they say good-bye."

He and his sister worked all afternoon to gather up the toys they hadn't looked at in years so they could be tossed away.

They played a checkers game that had no reds. They dealt out cards with every jack torn. And then she said, "Hey, look at this!" She pulled something out: It was the dollhouse. Inside was the soldier, the baker, and the airplane man, fallen together in a jumble.

"You used to play with them for hours," she said.

"When I was little," he said.

But now she had a far-off look in her eyes. "I used to play with them, too," she said. "They used to tell me wonderful things."

"And then they stopped?" he said.

"Then they stopped," she said.

For a while, they sat there together, passing the figures between them. There was a chipped spot on the baker, and the airplane man was smaller than they remembered.

Then they put them with the other toys.

That night, after his sister went to sleep, Charles got up from his bed and went downstairs into the hall, where the toys were stacked, waiting to be taken to the trash. He picked up the little pilot, seated in his plane. He zoomed him around, but the figure remained still and silent in his hands. His shoulders sank. It was silly, of course. But before he went to bed, he took some chalk, and wrote on a scrap of paper,

He taped it to the wall above their little house, as if it were written on the sky there. Then he put back the pilot and his plane.

After Charles climbed the stairs to his bedroom, the soldier, the baker, and the airplane man rose up from where they'd fallen.

"Let's go outside," said the soldier.

"Yes, let's," said the baker man.

They moved out of the little house, and when they looked up, they saw the words written there, as if they were painted on the sky.

"Look," said the baker.

"Yes, look," said the soldier. "Did you do that?" he said to the airplane man.

"No," said the airplane man. "The other one did—who used to play with us."

"Oh, yes," said the baker man.

"We haven't seen him in so long," said the soldier.

"We haven't seen her," said the baker man, "for even longer."

"But *he* did that," said the pilot. "So maybe he's coming back."

"And then we can fly like we used to!" they said.

"Yes, let's flyyyy!"

The next morning, Charles woke before dawn. All night long, he'd dreamed of a plane forming letters in the golden air. It took him to fabulous lands where warm breezes blew and everything shone with diamond light. And his sister was whispering through the wind, telling him she'd been there, too.

Coming downstairs, rubbing the sleep from his eyes, he saw the empty hall, the curtains blowing in, and he heard something outside.

It was the buzz of a motor.

He ran from his house, his heart beating. The sky was golden like that in his dream, with wisps of clouds like letters. He searched the sky, looking for the plane. He heard the motor start up again, quite near to him. It took him a moment to know what it was: A truck was coming for the trash, and the men were emptying the boxes and cans into its grinding gears.

All at once, Charles thought of the men in the little house. He ran to the trash bin. As the truck pulled near, he reached past ripped cards, the games with pieces missing, until, there! He pulled it out, with the baker, the soldier, and the airplane man inside.

"I've got you back," he said, looking down at them, as a man came over and emptied the bin. "We almost lost you."

But of course they didn't answer him, and after a moment, he understood why. In a corner of the sky, an airplane dipped its wings and was gone.

But as he clutched the little house, he understood that he hadn't brought it out for him, nor for her—he'd gotten it for someone else. And of course they were silent; they were saving up their words.

"I'll show you to him," he said to the little men. "To my new little brother." One by one, he picked them up in his hands, staring for a moment at each. "I wonder where you'll take him."

As Charles walked back to his house, with the little house under his arm, and the sun glinting off the windshields of cars, the words suddenly came to him: "Here we go!" he cried. And all at once, he did have a feeling of being in a new land, where everything was warm, and little people could suddenly grow tall.